CI N

A LITTLE PRINCESS

FRANCES HODGSON BURNETT

ADAPTED BY ANNE ROONEY · ILLUSTRATED BY DAVID SHEPHARD

NEW BURLINGTON BOOKS

From India to London

Sara Crewe had just arrived from India. She leaned her head against her father's shoulder as their carriage clattered through the London streets. The yellow fog hanging over London made the day as dark as night. She was shocked at the contrast between the hot country she had known all her life and the cold one she had come to.

"Papa," she said. "Is this the place?"

"Yes, little Sara," he answered. "It is."

Sara's mother had died when Sara was born, and she had always lived with her father. Sara had known that she would be sent to school in England when she was old enough. And, at seven, she finally was.

They drew up in front of a big, dull house with a brass plate that read, 'Miss Minchin, School for Young Ladies'. Captain Crewe lifted his daughter from the carriage and they went inside.

"I don't like it, Papa," Sara said. Everything was square, hard, ugly and unfriendly. When Miss Minchin came in, Sara felt she suited the house – she looked unfriendly, too.

"It will be wonderful to have such a beautiful and clever student," Miss Minchin said. Sara thought it was an odd thing to say, as she did not think herself beautiful and Miss Minchin did not yet know if she was clever.

Captain Crewe said that Sara was to have everything she wanted, including her own maid, carriage, fine clothes and the best rooms.

Sara told Miss Minchin that her best friend would be Emily.

"Who is Emily?" Miss Minchin asked. Sara replied that Emily was the perfect doll, but she did not have her yet.

"What an original child," Miss Minchin said, smiling at her coldly.

Sara stayed with her father in his hotel while he was in London. Every day, they went shopping to buy her beautiful clothes with frills and furs and feathers. They went from shop to shop in search of Emily, until at last they found her. And then they bought Emily lots of lovely clothes, too.

On his last day, Captain Crewe took Sara back to Miss Minchin's and said goodbye. She sat at the window of her lovely rooms watching until his carriage was out of sight. Miss Minchin sent her sister, Miss Amelia, to see what Sara was doing. But she had locked the door.

"I want to be quite by myself, if you please," Sara said. Miss Minchin was relieved that Sara did not shout and cry as she had expected such a spoiled child to do. And, although she thought Sara's clothes ridiculous, she looked forward to showing her off as the richest pupil in school.

The other girls at the school had heard about Sara's arrival and there were rumours about her lovely clothes and luxurious rooms. They all turned to watch as she walked to her place on the first day of lessons.

Miss Minchin's School

Miss Minchin introduced Sara to the class and then said, "As your papa has employed a French maid for you, I expect he wants you to learn French." She gave Sara a very simple book of French words.

"I have not learned French, but..." Sara began. She wanted to explain that her mother had been French, but Miss Minchin stopped her.

"That is enough. It is time you began."

When the French teacher arrived, Miss Minchin told him Sara was reluctant. But Sara spoke to him quickly in perfectly fluent French.

"Ah, Madame," the teacher said to Miss Minchin. "There is not much I can teach her – she *is* French. Her accent is delightful."

Miss Minchin was furious that Sara had made her look foolish. From then onwards, she didn't like Sara.

A sad-looking, plump girl called Ermengarde watched the drama unfold, anxiously chewing her pigtail. Miss Minchin soon told her off, and Sara felt sorry for her. She later learned that Ermengarde's father was always disappointed in her as she was not very clever. Sara promised to help her and Ermengarde cheered up considerably.

"Is it true," Ermengarde asked, "that you have your own playroom?"

"Yes," said Sara. "I make up stories when I play, but I don't like people to hear."

Sara took Ermengarde to her room to meet Emily, who Ermengarde thought the most beautiful doll she had ever seen. Sara told her she liked to imagine that when no one was around, dolls could move and talk and act just like little girls. Ermengarde spent the happiest hour of her entire life in Sara's room.

Sara was always kind and delightful and generous to everyone around her. But her good fortune annoyed two people. One was Miss Minchin, who thought her spoiled, but useful for showing off as a star pupil. The other was Lavinia, who was jealous of Sara. She had been Miss Minchin's favourite and the most popular girl in the school before Sara arrived.

The younger children especially loved Sara. She was kind about their troubles and tantrums.

"If you are four, you are four," she said to Lavinia, who had slapped little Lottie and called her a 'brat'. "But soon you will be too old for silly tantrums."

One day, Sara heard Miss Minchin and Miss Amelia trying to calm Lottie, who was wailing, "I haven't got a mamma!" The two women were cross and despairing in turn and it didn't help at all. Sara asked if she might try to calm Lottie. Instead of fussing, she sat quietly while Lottie cried. At last she told Lottie that she didn't have a mother either. She promised to be Lottie's mother while she was at school. Lottie quickly calmed down.

The Little Princess

Sara had been at Miss Minchin's school for two years when she caught sight of a dirty, smudgy face watching her as she went to her carriage dressed in her furs. That evening, she saw the very same girl come into the schoolroom carrying a box of coal. The tiny servant girl spent as long as she could making up the fire so that she could stay and listen as Sara told a story about a mermaid. All the girls, even Lavinia, could not help crowding round to listen to Sara's stories in the evenings. When Sara noticed the girl listening, she raised her voice so that the servant girl could hear more easily. All at once, the girl dropped a brush.

"That servant has been listening!" said Lavinia. But Sara did not mind at all. She believed that stories belonged to everyone.

Later Sara discovered from her maid, Mariette, that the little girl was Becky, the lowest servant in the house. Becky was always sent to run errands in the cold. She was always hungry and filthy from making up the fires.

A few weeks later, Sara came back from a dance class dressed in a rose pink dress with real matching roses in her hair. She opened the door to her room and found the little servant sleeping in a chair in front of the fire.

"Oh!" cried Sara, when she saw her. "You poor thing!"

Becky always saved cleaning Sara's room until last, as it was the prettiest and was full of lovely, interesting things. But today she was so exhausted that she had rested for a moment in Sara's soft, comfy chair – and then fallen fast asleep. When Becky opened her eyes, she saw Sara in her beautiful dress.

"Oh, Miss!" she cried, straightening her cap and jumping to her feet. "I didn't mean to! The fire was so warm, and I was so cold and tired…"

Sara put a hand on her shoulder and laughed kindly.

"Ain't you very angry, Miss?" Becky asked, afraid that Sara would tell Miss Minchin.

"Why, no," Sara said. "We are just the same. I am only a little girl like you. It is just an accident that I am not you and you are not me!"

Becky did not really understand, but Sara sat her down, gave her some cake and began to chatter to her.

Becky said Sara's dress made her look like a princess. Sara told her that she sometimes pretended to be a princess, and always tried to behave like one. Then she told her more of the mermaid story Becky had overheard. She promised to tell her a bit more of the story every day if Becky came to her room after she finished her work.

After Becky had gone, Sara murmured to herself, "If I were a real princess, I could give money and presents to everyone. As a pretend princess, I shall be kind to people instead."

Kind Deeds

A little time later, a letter came from Captain Crewe explaining that he was investing in some diamond mines with an old friend. It was going to make him very rich. Everyone in the school was excited, except for Lavinia and her friend Jessie. Lavinia didn't believe there were such things as diamond mines. Jessie told her that she'd heard Sara liked to pretend she was a princess, and they both laughed spitefully.

"I suppose she'd think she was a princess even if she were a beggar," Lavinia laughed.

When Lavinia and Jessie mocked Sara, she told them that pretending to be a real princess helped her to be kind to people.

Sara saw Becky every day. She began to buy Becky treats to eat as she was always so thin and hungry. Slowly, Becky grew plumper, healthier and happier. She was made to work harder as she grew stronger, but she felt she could put up with anything because she could look forward to spending time with Sara at the end of the day.

When it was nearly Sara's birthday, a letter came for her from her father. Captain Crewe was unwell, but he had sent instructions to Miss Minchin for Sara's birthday, and said that Sara must choose a doll. Sara said it would be her 'Last Doll', as at eleven she was almost too big for dolls. Miss Minchin bought all the things that Captain Crewe asked for – the doll, fine clothes and a birthday tea.

A Terrible Shock

When Sara's birthday arrived, the whole school went into Miss Minchin's sitting room for the tea party, and Miss Minchin made a speech about what a wonderful pupil Sara was. Miss Minchin saw Becky listening, and tried to send her away.

"Please may Becky stay?" Sara asked.

Miss Minchin was horrified.

"But she is a scullery maid!" she said. However, to please Sara, she let Becky stay.

Sara opened her presents. She had books, clothes, jewellery and the beautiful new doll. But just then, Miss Amelia came in.

"Sara, your papa's lawyer has come to see Miss Minchin," she said, "so you must all run along."

Everyone rushed away, but Becky stayed to look at the presents a moment too long. Just as she was about to leave, Miss Minchin came in with the lawyer, Mr Barrow. In a panic, Becky hid under a table, and from there she heard everything.

Mr Barrow told Miss Minchin that the diamond mines had failed and Captain Crewe had lost all his money before he died.

"He died!" cried Miss Minchin.

"Yes. And he lost every penny he had. He was already ill with jungle fever when he heard the news about the diamond mines, and the shock killed him. Sara is left penniless, and in your care."

Miss Minchin turned white with rage.

"I have been robbed and cheated! I will turn her out to live in the street!" she shouted.

"I wouldn't do that, Madam," Mr Barrow said. "It wouldn't look good for the school. Better keep her and make use of her as a servant."

Miss Minchin called Miss Amelia and told her to tell Sara the news and send her to put on a black dress. Then she sat and considered how much she had just spent on Sara's birthday – money that she would never be paid back.

When Sara appeared in front of Miss Minchin a few hours later, her face was white with dark rings under her eyes. She had listened to the news from Miss Amelia without speaking, and then run to her room where she repeated over and over, "My papa is dead! My papa is dead!"

Now she stood, clutching Emily, as Miss Minchin told her she would have no time for dolls in the future. She would work as a servant and do everything she was told.

"You are a beggar now – not a princess!" Miss Minchin said. "You have no relations, no home, no one to care for you. You can stay here but you must work."

Sara ran from the room, but Miss Amelia stopped her going into her own bedroom.

"This is not your room now. You must sleep in the attic next to Becky's room," she said.

A Strange New Life

As she closed the door behind her, Sara's heart sank. This was another world. The room had a slanting roof with a skylight, and the whitewash was peeling off the walls. There was nothing but a hard bed and a few pieces of battered furniture. Sara sat on a footstool, laid Emily over her lap and cried.

After a short time, there was a tap at the door, and Becky came in. She too had been crying.

"Oh, Becky," Sara said. "I told you we were just the same. You see how true it is? I'm no princess any more."

"Yes, you are!" Becky cried. "Whatever happens to you, nothing could make you different!"

The first night Sara spent in the attic was a night she never forgot. She felt sadder than she had ever felt in her life. She tossed and turned, trying to get comfortable, and whispered over and over to herself, "My papa is dead!" The wind howled in the darkness and Sara heard shuffling and squeaking in the walls. She knew it was mice and rats. She lay trembling, with the covers pulled over her head.

Sara's life changed all at once. Her maid Mariette was sent away, and from the very next morning, Sara had to sit at breakfast with the smallest children and help them. She was sent on errands and had chores heaped on her by the servants, who rather enjoyed ordering around the girl they had been forced to make a fuss over before.

For the first few months, Sara thought that if she showed willing, the servants might be kinder to her. But she soon realized that this wasn't true – they simply gave her more tasks and scolded her. She no longer had lessons, but studied alone at the end of the day – she was afraid she would forget what she had learned if she did not study.

Miss Minchin didn't like Sara to talk to the other girls.

"To think that she was the girl with the diamond mines!" Lavinia scoffed. "Doesn't she look odd now!"

Sara worked harder than ever. She tramped through cold, wet streets carrying parcels, and grew shabbier and more miserable every day. She had to eat her meals downstairs with the servants. Although her heart was breaking, she told herself, "Soldiers don't complain, and I shan't. I shall pretend this is a war."

There were times when Sara thought her heart might break of loneliness if it were not for her few friends. Becky still helped Sara whenever she could. And, one day, Sara went up to her attic room at the end of the day and found Ermengarde there waiting for her. Ermengarde looked around the tiny, bare room.

"Oh Sara, how can you bear living here?" she asked, sorrowfully.

Sara started to feel a little more like her old self as her imagination began to work.

"If I pretend it's quite different, I can," she said. "Or if I pretend it is a place in a story."

Melchisedec

Lottie was also a good friend to Sara. She was too small to understand what had happened and Sara didn't want to tell her. But, one day, Lottie climbed the stairs to Sara's room to find out for herself.

"Sara!" she cried, horrified that the room was so bare and ugly. Sara was worried that Lottie would make a fuss and be discovered.

"It's not so bad," she said quickly. "Look, you can see all sorts of things from the window." She showed Lottie the view from the skylight and a tiny sparrow hopping about. They fed some crumbs to the sparrow, and Sara helped her to imagine how lovely the room could be if there were a fire in the grate and comfortable furniture. When Lottie had gone, though, the room felt cold and empty again.

"It's sometimes the loneliest place in the world," Sara said to herself. At that moment, she heard a little sound, and looked up. There, sitting sniffing the air, was a large rat.

"I dare say it's rather hard to be a rat," Sara said. "Nobody likes you. But it's not your fault you were born a rat." She sat very still, and eventually the rat crept up and ate some of the crumbs that Lottie had dropped on the floor. Sara decided to call him Melchisedec and make him a friend.

"After all," she thought, "prisoners made friends with rats."

The Indian Gentleman

When Sara had been rich and finely dressed, everyone had admired her when she went out. Now, no one looked at her at all, and feeling invisible made her lonelier than ever. Instead, she watched other people. She liked to look into one nearby house in particular. It belonged to a family she called the Large Family, because there were eight children. One day, as she watched them get into their carriage, one of the boys turned towards her.

"Here, poor little girl, here's a sixpence for you."

Sara suddenly realized that she looked just like the poor children on the street. She didn't want to take the sixpence, but she saw it would make the boy happy, so she did. She thanked him so politely that the Large Family children were puzzled.

"She can't be a beggar," one of the girls said. They were so interested in her after that that they watched out for her, and called her 'the little girl who is not a beggar'. Sara made a hole in the sixpence and hung it around her neck.

The house next to Miss Minchin's had been empty for years. Sara longed for someone to move in. How nice it would be if a friendly head could pop out of the skylight next to hers and wish her good morning! Then, one day, she saw men carrying crates and furniture into the house. Some of the furniture looked Indian. What a lovely sight!

That night, Becky came to Sara's room with news.

"It's an Indian gentleman," she said. "He's very rich, and he's ill, and the father of the Large Family is his lawyer!"

It was a few weeks before the Indian gentleman moved in. He had no wife or children, only a nurse and two servants. He looked sick, was very thin and was always wrapped in furs.

Some time later, Sara was standing on the table looking at the sunset out of the skylight, when she saw a head at the next window. It was brown-skinned and wearing a turban. She smiled at the man, and he smiled back but, as he did so, he accidentally let go of a little monkey he was holding. It ran across the roof and jumped through Sara's skylight!

Sara had learned to speak Hindustani when she lived in India, and spoke it now to the man to ask if the monkey would let her catch him. The man was called Ram Dass and was the servant, or lascar, as they were sometimes known, of the Indian gentleman. They decided it would be best if he crawled across the roof and caught the monkey himself. Despite the shabby attic, Ram Dass treated Sara with all the respect she was used to from her servants in India.

After he had gone, she thought about what had happened. She straightened her thin little body, and said, "Even if I am dressed in rags and tatters, I can still be a princess inside."

The Other Side of the Wall

Sara grew fond of the new gentleman next door, even without meeting him. She learned that he was English, but had lived in India for a long time. He had fallen ill after some bad luck with diamond mines.

In turn, the gentleman, whose name was Mr Carrisford, learned a little about Sara. The children of the Large Family told him about the 'little girl who is not a beggar', and Ram Dass described the adventure with the monkey. He called his lawyer, the father of the Large Family, Mr Carmichael, over for a talk.

"Hearing about the poor girl next door has made me worry that Crewe's child – the child I never stop thinking about – could be in a similar state," he said.

"If the child is in Paris, as you believe, I am sure she is well looked after," Mr Carmichael replied.

"I am not *sure* she is in Paris!" he worried. "I only think that because her mother was a Frenchwoman. I *must* find her. Crewe was my oldest friend and his child might be begging in the street. He put every penny he had into the diamond mines, and he died thinking I had lost his money!"

"Come, come," Carmichael reassured him. "You were ill at the time, too, and could not tell him the mines had had a change of luck or ask about his daughter. We shall find the child and you will have a fortune to hand to her. I have a new lead. I will travel to Moscow and look for her there."

A Secret Feast

The winter was bleak, and Sara suffered cruelly. One day, she found a silver coin in the mud. Sara was hungrier than ever and crossed the road to the bakers. But, on the way, she spotted a beggar child with eyes even hungrier than her own. Sara bought six hot buns and gave five of the buns to the cold and starving child.

"She is hungrier than I am," she said to herself.

When she got home, she saw the children of the Large Family saying goodbye to Mr Carmichael as he set off to travel to Russia.

"If you find the little girl, Father, give her our love," shouted one of them.

I wonder who the little girl is, thought Sara.

While Sara had been out, Mr Carrisford had asked his secretary and Ram Dass to sneak across the roof and go into Sara's attic room. They measured, and took notes, and saw how shabby it was.

"Do you think it can be done while she sleeps?" the secretary asked Ram Dass.

"I can move as if my feet were velvet," he replied.

They slipped away, and when Sara returned that evening there was no sign they had ever been there. She was late for dinner, and the cook gave her a piece of stale bread. As Sara climbed the steps to the attic room, she saw a light under her door and found Ermengarde waiting for her. Sara was glad, but Ermengarde did not really understand how terrible Sara's life was.

As Sara and Ermengarde talked, they heard Miss Minchin shouting at Becky for stealing a meat pie. Becky was muttering that she hadn't stolen the pie, though she would have liked to – she was so hungry.

Ermengarde opened her eyes wide in horror.

"Sara, are *you* ever hungry?"

Sara was just too tired to pretend.

"Yes," she said, "I'm so hungry now I could eat you!"

Ermengarde jumped up.

"I'm so silly!" she cried. "My aunt sent me a box of lovely treats to eat! I'll go back to my room and get it!"

Sara went to fetch Becky and they pretended that they were decorating a huge banquet hall. When Ermengarde returned, they spread all the wonderful things to eat on a shawl that served as a tablecloth.

Suddenly, Miss Minchin burst into the room, white with anger. She hit Becky, and shouted at her.

"Go to your room immediately!"

She made Ermengarde take the treats away, and told Sara she would have no food the next day. Sara gazed at her, saying nothing, and this angered Miss Minchin.

"What are you thinking?" she demanded.

"I was wondering," Sara answered, "what my papa would say if he knew where I am tonight."

"You insolent child!" Miss Minchin shouted, shaking her violently. "Go to bed this instant!"

As Sara went sadly to bed, a head peered in unnoticed through the skylight.

A Perfect Surprise

Sara lay down to sleep, imagining she had soft downy pillows and fleecy blankets. When she was woken a little while later by a sound, she felt too warm and snug to open her eyes. She was having a delightful dream that she was covered with a satin quilt and she didn't want to wake up. When at last she did open her eyes, she couldn't believe them.

"I am still dreaming!" she whispered. She *was* covered by a satin quilt. A fire was burning in the grate, a little kettle hissed on the hob and a thick, warm rug lay on the floor. There were blankets and a little folding chair and table. On the table a wonderful meal was spread out, with a teapot ready to be filled. She touched everything and it was real. There was even a note that read 'To the little girl in the attic. From a friend'.

Sara rushed to Becky's room and dragged her over to see the wonderful changes. They had a feast of soup, sandwiches, muffins, toast and tea, and it was all real.

"Do you think it could melt away, Miss?" Becky asked, cramming a sandwich into her mouth, just in case. At last, warm and fed, they shared the blankets between them and both went back to bed.

"If it ain't here in the morning," Becky said as she went off to her own room, "at least it was here tonight. And I'll never forget it!"

The Surprise Continues

But everything was still there in the morning. And, as the days passed, more and more wonderful things appeared while Sara was out or sleeping. Delicious, hot food – enough for her and Becky – arrived every morning and night.

The weather got worse and worse, and the cook sent Sara on more errands outside. Lavinia sneered at Sara's clothes, which got shabbier and shabbier. But Sara remained cheerful, happy in the knowledge that she had a secret friend watching out for her somewhere.

Miss Minchin had expected Sara and Becky to be miserable after she had told them off for eating Ermengarde's food, and she was puzzled that they were both increasingly cheerful. They even seemed to look better fed and healthier, though they were given so little food it should not have been possible. Miss Minchin took this as an insult.

"Sara Crewe looks well," she said to Miss Amelia. She was becoming suspicious – how could Sara look so healthy on such ill treatment?

A few days later, Sara went to answer a knock on the door. A man handed over a pile of parcels all addressed to 'The little girl in the right-hand attic'. As Miss Minchin was passing, she told Sara to take the parcels directly to the girl they were for.

"They are for me," Sara said. Miss Minchin looked at the label in confusion and told Sara to open the parcels.

The parcels were filled with pretty, comfortable clothes, including shoes, stockings and a warm coat. There was a note pinned to them which read, 'To be worn every day. Will be replaced when necessary'.

Miss Minchin was disturbed and worried. Could she, she wondered, have been wrong about Sara? Perhaps the girl had some unknown rich relative. A rich relative would not like the way Sara was now being treated.

"Well," Miss Minchin said, "you had better go and put them on. No need for any more errands today."

When Sara walked into the schoolroom half an hour later, the other pupils were struck dumb. They were even more surprised when Miss Minchin told Sara to sit in her old place.

"Perhaps the diamond mines have appeared again," said Lavinia, bitterly.

That night, Sara had an idea. Among the things that had appeared in her room was a writing set. So she wrote a thank you note to the kind friend who was leaving her presents and left it with the tea things.

The next evening, the note had gone. But something else appeared. Sara and Becky heard a scratching at the skylight – it was the monkey again. Sara let him in. It was far too cold for the monkey to be outside, but too late to take him home.

"I shall let him sleep with me tonight, and take him back to the Indian gentleman tomorrow," Sara said.

Returning the Monkey

The next day, the Large Family were at Mr Carrisford's house awaiting the return of Mr Carmichael from Moscow. He brought bad news.

"She is not the child we are looking for," he said. "The girl I found is much younger than Captain Crewe's daughter."

"The search must start again!" Mr Carrisford said.

"She must be somewhere," said Mr Carmichael. "Let us give up on Paris. Let us start in London."

"There are lots of schools in London," Mr Carrisford said. "There is a sad little girl in the one next door. She is as unlike the Crewe girl as any child could be."

At that moment, Ram Dass came in to say that the little girl from next door had just arrived.

"Your monkey ran away again," Sara said, stepping into the room. "Shall I give him to the lascar?"

"How do you know he is a lascar?" asked Mr Carrisford, astonished.

"Oh, I know what lascars are," Sara explained to him. "I was born in India."

Mr Carrisford sat up suddenly, with a strange expression on his face. Sara told him that she had been brought to Miss Minchin's as a pupil, but when her father died she had been left a beggar.

"How did your father lose his money?" he asked.

"He had a friend he trusted too much," Sara replied. "His friend took his money for the diamond mines."

Mr Carrisford could not believe his ears.

"What was your father's name?" he asked. "Tell me."

"Ralph Crewe," Sara answered.

"It is the child – the child!" he cried.

The whole story came tumbling out. Sara learned that Mr Carrisford had not cheated her papa at all, but had genuinely thought he had lost all the money. He had fallen ill with fever, and by the time he recovered, Captain Crewe was dead. Mr Carrisford had been searching for Sara ever since.

"And, all the while, I was just the other side of the wall," whispered Sara.

At that moment, Miss Minchin came in. She had seen Sara go into the house and had followed her to apologize for the disturbance.

"She is not going back with you," Mr Carrisford said sternly.

Mr Carmichael explained everything to Miss Minchin, who felt it was the worst thing that had ever happened to her. When she heard that Sara was, after all, to inherit a huge fortune from the diamond mines, she made one last attempt to win her back.

"Her father left her in my care," she said. "If it weren't for me, she would have starved in the street."

"She would have been better off in the street than starving in your attic!" Mr Carrisford said. "Sara, how would you like to live here with me from now on?"

Of course, Sara gratefully accepted Mr Carrisford's offer. Miss Minchin stormed home to find Miss Amelia. But Miss Amelia turned on her.

"I am always afraid to say things to you for fear of making you angry," she said, "but you should have been less severe on Sara Crewe. She was a good child, and too clever for you. She saw that you were hard-hearted and that I was a fool. And all the time she behaved like a little princess!"

That evening the other girls in the school found out what was going on. Ermengarde brought in a letter from Sara that explained everything.

"There *were* diamond mines!" she said at last.

When Becky went up to her attic room that night, Ram Dass was waiting for her with a letter. She was to move to Mr Carrisford's house and live with Sara.

Sara did not forget what it felt like to be poor. The next day, she asked to go to the shop where she had once bought six buns. The woman in the shop remembered Sara giving away five of her buns to a hungry little girl. Sara said that she would like to pay for bread and buns for all the poor children who came to the shop from then onwards.

"Do you know where the little girl is now?" Sara asked.

"Why, she is here! She works for me," the woman said.

"Then let her be the one to give bread and buns to the poor children!" Sara said. And as she and Mr Carrisford rode away in the carriage, Sara felt happy.

About the author

Born in Manchester, England, in 1849, Frances Eliza Hodgson was the eldest daughter in a large family. As a young girl she scrawled stories on old sheets of paper, as she could not afford proper writing materials. In 1865, the family moved to Tennessee, USA, and Frances began to send her stories to women's magazines. She wrote her first children's book, *Little Lord Fauntleroy*, in 1886 and based the main character on her youngest son. After her eldest son, Lionel, died tragically in 1890, Frances moved to New York, where she wrote her two most famous stories – *A Little Princess* and *The Secret Garden*. She became very eccentric in her old age and died in 1924.

Other titles in the Classic Collection series:

Alice's Adventures in Wonderland • *Little Women*
The Three Musketeers • *Treasure Island* • *Pinocchio*
20,000 Leagues Under the Sea • *Heidi* • *The Wizard of Oz*
Robinson Crusoe • *Robin Hood* • *Tom Sawyer* • *Gulliver's Travels*
The Secret Garden • *Anne of Green Gables* • *Black Beauty*

A NEW BURLINGTON BOOK
The Old Brewery
6 Blundell Street
London N7 9BH

QED Project Editor: Alexandra Koken
Managing Editor: Victoria Garrard • Design Manager: Anna Lubeka
Editor: Louise John • Designer: Rachel Clark

First published in the UK in 2013 by
QED Publishing, A Quarto Group company,
230 City Road, London EC1V 2TT

www.qed-publishing.co.uk

A catalogue record for this book is available from the British Library.

ISBN 978 1 78171 350 1

Printed in China